LEARNING To Read While Getting Drunk

William Ardrey

A Look Inside

The ole professor claimed he had a reason for howling. I asked what could excuse such behavior. He told me he had been borne at home, on a ranch in Montana.

"What's so unusual about that" I had to ask. He sniffed to show he knew how, and then replied,

"The only doctor available was a veterinarian and that has weight heavily on my mind all these years. Being delivered by a Vet, is disgracing. When I get loaded I start to look wall-eyed and howl".

I just gave him the rest of the jug and let him go into never-never land. That would keep old Rover quite for a while. Next morning he was led back to wino alley, I thought he wanted to be among his own kind. Lesson learned; you cannot learn much from a professor, if he is a drunken Wino.

A THOUGHT:

"A sign of an educated mind is one that entertains an idea without necessarily accepting it". Aristotle

Other Books by William Ardrey

Wade Explains Ranch Life

The Old Cowboys: Love To Make Money

Star Truck

How I got Fat

Learning To Read

The Old Cowboys: We Go North

My Very Good Luck

Red Meat: The Doctor

The Big Bang Revisited

Gold Wolf

The Wrath Of The Grapes

The Trouble Shooters

CONTENT

Chapter 1

"Read any good books lately"? That was a question, on a T.V. game show. Seeing that got me to thinking, how long had it been since I had read a good book. Realizing because of too much watching TV, I didn't even know how to read. I wanted to remedy the oversight? Just to be sure, there wasn't something wrong with me, I went **to a doctor.** It seemed the right thing to do. And while sitting in the lobby, I picked up a magazine, looked at the pictures and sighed. During my office visit, there was some explaining to the doctor. Suddenly while sitting in the patient chair, everything went black I was unconscious. I woke up around 2 am cold, and wet. Realizing my surroundings, I was in wino alley, skid row part of town. Several winos were steadily giving me the eye. They were looking hungrily at me as if I were a rare T-Bone. Not saying anything, I just looked back at them. Truthfully, I was a little bit in awe of them too. They must have figured out I wasn't a bottle of wine, or didn't have any wine, so they went and sat down. That crazy

Doctor had drugged me and robbed me of everything in my possession. My lips felt large and numb, he had pulled all my gold teeth. The teeth bought after hitting the lottery, that one time.

Talk about a sleazy guy, man he was. This robbery now told me, how he was able to run his free clinic. But because he had a lot of political friends; I just had to let it slide, and would wait until I had some influence in city hall. But in reality thinking to myself, who I am kidding?

As usual, I also wondered how to face the future. And while that thinking, was going on, up popped the past. The past still haunted me. I didn't actually do the deed but, suffered for it. Once in a weak moment at 6 years old, I thought about voting for a democrat, also wanting to grow up and be a responsible citizen. The brief moment, of that one impure thought then, still haunted me now. Having a 105 degree fever brought on by the measles, and a bad cold was no excuse. In one of my conscious moments, they told me; "the thought police" would be coming for me on Tuesday."

It didn't occur to me there was no such thing. My older brother was the bearer of the sad tidings. He had told me, even though my fever was still a raging furnace; it didn't matter if I was sick, they were coming for me. He did give me a recommendation,

"Running away from home at your age is sort of risky, but you had better go".

He must have told my parents and God it was my idea, to leave.

Getting away meant hiding by day and cringing by night, it was tough. And how did I get my education? By standing outside people's windows and watching their T.V. The people on the T.V shows seemed weird but, how could one so young be sure. There were no friends, to talk to, and on the run, from the thought police. Living, by hunting and foraging was a good idea two hundred years ago but a rough way to go these days. Rough as it was I finally got a little older, and began to control my thoughts, somewhat.

Now, being hard headed, I am more determined than ever to learn how to read. And even though it might mean going to a crazy doctor, I needed answers. Realizing that being able to

read, might ward off any more medical mishaps.
Hell, that might not even, have been a doctor,
I went to. He might have been some kind of
crook.

Now as usual, I was friendless, and alone, in
an alley filled with red-eyed winos. Some of
them resembled the awful Gargoyles, on the
public buildings. However, what could be done?
Right now any talking was difficult because of
my recent dental work. That dam crazy doctor
pulled almost, all my teeth, gold or not.
There were only a few teeth left. The winos
thought they were just seeing, another drunk,
or something. They were used to people who
could hardly speak. My mind was whirling,
trying to think. Who could I possibly trust in
times like these? Out of that alley I went,
as quickly as possible; they might be hungry,
who knew?

After a few weeks, of licking my wounds, and
hearing insults, there came an inspiration. At
a table in the city park, a kid sat reading
some book, if he could read, so could I. But
for now it was back to wino alley in the day
time, to make some friends. It was easy to
make them like me; I took some, vino to them.

I had found a sure fire easy way to get my wine supplies. Using the few tools in my possession, such as stealth, was the way. The ideas of a mangy street person, was all I knew.

Running into a large Liquor store and yelling; Fire! Fire!, Did the trick. The clerk ran out the front door, to see what was going on. I ran out the back door, with all the cases of wine that could possibly be carried. Several trips in rapid succession, and there was a sizeable stash out in the woods. Now I was set.

Armed with good ole vino made me a lot of "Friends", some I didn't want. I did not learn any more about reading; those mangy hounds would guzzle the wine as fast as they could. A half hour later those red-eyed dogs would go to sleep. And it is hard to learn anything, from a sleeping Wino. They just don't seem to know anything at all.

When the wine ran low, they started to get surly. Ole, 'Scar-Face" gave me a clue, when he started to tell me, "shut-up stupid".

Well, right then the honeymoon was over, and the worst was about to happen. As I, started to leave the area, one person followed me out of the wino alley. She was Chatty Kathy, one of the volunteer social workers that often visited the alley. She did volunteer work, part time for some place called Sally's Army. That Army was probably on some, "Dry out the Winos" campaign. Moreover, she kept following me, to my home away from home, my old shack in an abandon ruins area. We talked and talked and found out we had some things in common. She said she could read, and would teach me. But, how that was going to happen, was a complete mystery. Poor Ole Chatty Kathy was prone to speak with a pronounced lisp, and she stuttered quite a lot. Half the time I wasn't really sure what she said. But I would just say yes dear and uh huh, things like that. Chatty was kind of likeable, and there might be some chance for romance. Above all else, there might be a chance for, my learning to read. The Lisping and stuttering problem was over come. We found out that if she sang the words, written in a book, the lisping stopped. When she sang, my reading lessons I got every word. The local library had some song books, and that was a start. Now feeling better about life I wanted to get a job of some kind. And maybe get a driver's license, and learn to read the Bible, while driving my car. Me and ole Chatty shacked-up, in a nice little place she had, we were going steady, one could say. She was my one and only friend, besides them mangy old winos. They were not as sweet and nice as Chatty; they got too surly when the wine ran out. But who cares? Even with the speech thing, she was easier to understand than a drunken Wino. So we sang a lot, and the reading lessons were a wonderful blessing. By reading stories, the knowledge of why the cow jumped over the moon was revealed to me. Thinking there must be space cows, was somewhat new to me. And old Jack and Jill probably were shacking up too.

Chapter 2

Well it was bound to happen, once a wino always a wino. But don't, ya see, it is not my fault, I aint to blame for what happened. Blame it on my roots; some races are more prone to be a slave to the grape than others are. And the word, or the title, Wino-Alcoholic, whichever is the preferred way to say it, means the same.

Dear ole chatty liked to have a glass of vino with the evening meal; winos want a glass of wine, instead, of the meal. And that's what added up to my big time backsliding, better known as the "Relapse". When, al-key's, aka winos take one drink it sets up a craving, for the divine juice. And if they get their hands on a jug, nothing can keep them sober. Hell fire that damn vino, even got to Jesus Christ, every now and then. So we mere mortals, if we have the bug, don't stand a chance.

Fire! Fire! That was the warning, yelled by someone who had done it before. The clerk was still, silly enough to run out and see what was going on. And after several trips, to the woods, and back, were made; it netted a fair supply of Nectar. It was the kind of haul, most winos can only dream about. Because a real, down and out guzzler can't think that far in the future. I still did have some, sober thoughts.

Well I was back on skid row, in wino alley, guzzling the vino with the rest of the boys. There was one poor old woman lying around drunk, and it was bad. Men lying around wasted didn't look so bad, but that poor female creature did. It must be true, a few of the people that become drunks are mentally ill, but not all are. Now, if you use the medical term of, "Obsessive-Compulsive" they might be. But if you use that same medical term on big time bankers, and the other money men, you have to conclude they are, crazy as hell. I mean they are literally nutty. The rich have such an Obsessive-compulsion to amass money it is sickening to watch. And their obsession with that accumulation is nothing but criminal. Not all the mental cases, in the world, could commit the amount of crime the money boys do. Murder, Robbery, treason is every day thing to the crazy bankers. If that seems too hard to believe, well, a lot of people know it's true. One way to see the truth in anything is to apply the following questions to the idea.

Question 1; Do you think they got all that money, by sharing with others? Nope.

Question 2; Do they, want you, to have any? Nope, again.

Question 3. Who has the most to gain by you not believing, they are criminals?

It's simple, even a wino can figure it out.

I decided to go to the library and find some song books, the kind Chatty had shown me. It must have been a special day, or something there. It was probably a program, to get kids interested in reading. They had a children's room set up, in the back part of the building. One little girl was reading to her dog, its name was Gabby. And they both looked very serious, about learning the dog to read. The little girl was making sure that the dog was paying attention, by giving him a stern look, ever so often. And the dog was showing interest, and pretending he understood, by licking his chops, and changing his facial expression.

Well that was a low point in my life, knowing a dog could read better than me. At least he had found a teacher, I hadn't found another one yet. I borrowed some songbooks from the library and tried to practice my reading lessons. Because learning to read while staying drunk, is not easy. I kept forgetting the words to the song, and sometimes even the name of the song. Hells Fire!

Why did I eat that glass of wine, with ole Chatty, instead of eating my supper? I should have my backside kicked, and probably will. Going around ole mean Scar Face, when he runs low on wino Juice is dangerous. That started me to think; it would be better go to my other home, the shack among the ruins. Because the biggest part of my wine stash is there anyway. That way I can drag it out, and have a nice long drunk session. And there, would not be any of them damn mean Red eyed Gargoyles.

On the way to my hideout I met a collage professor. He was panhandling for spare change; he no doubt needed a little pick me up, aka vino. Yep the old boy was dry he said, and wanted some juice. I told him I had a small jug at my shack, and he was welcome to have a slug or two. He didn't know there was a new plan being formulated. I figured, he surly, could read. And the way he talked, he probably had written some books. After passing the jug around a few times, I asked about reading lessons. Sure, he said that he could help, and would be glad to further my education. We passed the nectar container around a few more times, and he got a faraway look in his eyes. He must have been in the advanced stages of alcoholism, it didn't take, all that much to load his wagon. And by now He already had too big of a load, to teach me anything, except how to howl, and talk nonsense. I was well versed on that howling stuff already, having experienced it, quite a few times myself. The ole professor claimed he had a very good reason for howling. I asked what could excuse such behavior. He told me he had been borne at home, on a ranch in Montana. "What's so unusual about that" I had to ask. He said "The only doctor available was a veterinarian and that has weight heavily on my mind all these years. Being, delivered by a Vet is disgracing. When I get loaded I start to look wall-eyed and howl."

I just gave him the rest of the jug and let him go into never-never land. That would keep old Rover quite for a while. Next morning, he was led back to wino alley. I thought he wanted to be among his own kind. Lesson learned; you cannot learn much from a professor, if he is a drunken Wino.

Having, gone three days without being drunk, I decided to go back to my other home, away from home. No not the shack in the ruins, I went to see my nice warm girlfriend Chatty. It's a good thing she was gone to work; it gave me time to do some house cleaning, to show her my repentance for going on a binge. Ole Cathy worked in the loan dept, at the bank. Heck she probably had made the bank a small fortune that day. The costumers that she talked to were the high-end depositors. Some of them, thought, her speech was real funny. And that lisp, ole chatty had, combined with her rapid fire way of speaking was, sort of amusing to them also. And if you add in the stuttering,

the recipe for jollies was there. The woman
was a good sport, and didn't mind their holier
than thou attitude at all. Every time they did
their snickering, she did her thing. Her way
of laughing was, jacking up the interest
rates, of the loans the Hyenas signed up for.
Of course, it was in print too small for the
Hubble telescope to see. And the words only
showed after the special laser was applied to
the document. But the law was clear, just like
everyone else, they had signed it. Chatty
Cathy had mastered the concept; "Don't get
mad, get even".
After doing some token house cleaning for
Chatty, I felt a nap was in order, sure wish I
hadn't done that napping. Even though I
showered very well, there was still some smell
of the wino juice on me. When a real boozer
sweats, it comes out of your pores, for a day
or two, or more.
When Chatty Cathy saw me napping on her couch
and caught the faint wine odor, the jig was
up. She must have thought I got drunk and
passed out. There is no way, you can convince
a woman, when their dander is up. They are
just like a bear; if you make a Grizzly mad, a

50 caliber machine gun has little effect on it. Well mama bear Chatty, was on fire, at least her hair was. She said, "Get out, and that I better stay gone".

In the old days women had to be slapped, to bring their thinking around. Back then it was a real struggle to just stay alive. And there was no time to talk to a hysterical, woman, so men took a short-cut. Back then it was done for their, own good. Because the treatment, also cut down on, their stroke producing anger. But, you know helping them that way, won't work now. That is because some laws have been passed that says, don't do that. And *the*se modern women would rather die of stroke or heart attack, than to be helped. Their number one killer today, is heart attacks. A lot of progress is made by mankind every day; I am not sure, which was worse.

There have been documented cases of women saying, "Don't tell me what to do."

Even when you are telling them grab a rope, that will prevent them drowning. Well they get their way, and that's important. Drowning to them is secondary.

Sadly it is historical fact one of the first,

self-made female billionaires, ole Hattie,
died of a stroke. She was arguing about the
value of skim milk. She did not want, to be
told anything.
There is a least one thing on that subject
worth knowing;
"You can be right, or you can be happy"
 your choice. But sadly some people have to be
right all the time to be happy anytime.

Chapter 3

So off into the wild blue yonder, I
went, because she wanted it that way. I didn't
give her any stroke prevention help; because
she did not, want it that way.
Being a real sound sleeper, and not knowing
how it happened; I woke up in Jail again.
After the shock of my surroundings wore off
some, I tried to piece it all together. Some
of the other occupants had been there, when
they brought me in, and deposited me in the
cell. Studying the wolves carefully before
making, any attempt to glean information,
seemed in order. One guy seemed to be boss of
the outfit; at least it looked that way. He
kept telling, this other, curly haired guy; it
was his time to mop the floor. Curly head
denied it was his time to swab the deck. They
went back and forth, yes it is, No it aint,
just like kids. I felt like throttling them
both, but didn't. Then they let it rest for a
few hours, all was quiet, and peaceful, in our
nice steel bar home. After about three new
sessions of that noise, I jumped up, grabbed

the Mop, to swab the deck. Maybe there would
be no choking the two nuts, but I could take
away their reason to make noise. Ole bossy guy
looked at me sort of innocent like and said,
 "You don't have to mop the floor".
Well I knew I didn't have to. They both in
turn, received a very hard stare from me. I
think they finally saw that a, hung-over
Juicer, is dangerous, with the headache and
all. The decision to not choke them was made;
instead, their throats were going to be ripped
like a wolf, had been at them. I am fairly
certain they saw that in my stare, and saw
their blood already dripping, from my muzzle.

        Still I did not know why or how long my
stay in Shangri-La had been. Nobody wanted to
talk to me; they saw I was dangerous, to
myself, more than anything else. I guess they,
at least had enough sense to know:
"When you find yourself in a hole stop
digging, you can get out faster that way".
Also it was about feeding time for us cage
dwellers, usually a time of reverence, and
contemplation.
Man was I drawing bad hands from lady luck. I
went from paradise with a beautiful woman that

had money to skid row, and now in the pits of
hell. My luck was due to change, and it did.
Man I really hated the change that came next.

No one could like, the little beady-eyed
Judge that did our arraignment. But it was
more like being peed on, than rained on. I
finally found out why I was a guest in
Crossbar hotel, armed robbery! Bail set at 50
grand cash! I hollered lord have mercy on me.
Right now, I didn't have even enough sense, to
crawl up the ladder to the level of stupid.
Not having any money and being in Jail is a
low station in life. If I was in the animal
world, it would be like being a, damn mangy
hog, or worse. I didn't start crying, having
out grown that behavior, years before. But
there were thoughts of getting relief somehow.
Making it known I didn't have any money for an
attorney, was smart of me. They were nice
enough to furnish one.
That free Lawyers eyes looked red, as if he
had been boozing as much as me. However, there
was no need to get uppity with him because, he
was my link to the outside world. A place I
hoped to see again, someday. The best thing I
could think of, was sending a letter to dear

Sweet Chatty.

My public defender had a document he wanted me to read and sign. I explained to him I couldn't read that well. He got a look in his eye that resembled a tightwad, saving a quarter, on something. Those eyes were lit up like a search light. Something had to done something quick, Beady-eyes was going to sell me down the river.

Somewhere he found out if he cut short, his time with me, he could get back to the Bar Association meetings, at Joes bar downtown. Luckily I got one of the other inmates to write me a letter, and asked the Beady-eyed Lawyer to deliver it to Chatty.

And when I talked to beady eyes, I stressed that I wanted to get out of Jail, and would get out someday. I think he noticed my train of thought. Approaching my darkest hour it happened, light at the tunnel end. My Dear sweet Cathy, came riding to the rescue, and offered a peace treaty. I was so glad to see that woman, in many ways. Them, mangy roommates I was bunked with were a motley crew, to put it mildly. Also I was, genuinely fond of Chatty. No, that, wasn't exactly true,

By-God I loved that woman. And there was no hesitating to tell her, that I did. Being a respectable Lady, and employed, she had influence. Also she was well acquainted with, Mr. Dollar Bill.

Love might make the world go around, but as they say, ole Bill greases the wheels. I was expecting to get a lecture about my errant ways, but no, she didn't do that. She was glad to see me too. Looking at that angel of mercy, I vowed to try, and do better, so help me.

Chapter 4

Chatty had enough influence to get me a real lawyer instead of ole Beady-Eyes. Now not all public defenders were that anxious, to float you on into the pen, but ole Beady eyes, was that kind. Someday, I said to myself, he will get in a jam, and the way he works, it might be soon. Some of those crooks that he is selling out, will get out, and he might go under. That is if his boozing didn't get him first. Good riddance you son-of-a-gun.
I still had to see the Judge and let him do his thing, make me or break me. That's a lot of power for one man, and it must have weighted heavy on him. Maybe that's why he drank so much booze. His face was red as a Beet all the time, and his nose had a big vein popping out. He was doing the same thing that I did; guzzle booze, only he got well paid for sending others to hell. The only reason, I think, that he got away with it, was because he could read, and I couldn't. My new, well

paid lawyer got the police to admit that, I
wasn't part of that armed robbery, as they
first claimed I was. They said it was all a
mistake. And that the real and only robber had
ran into my part of wino alley. They even
admitted that I was sound asleep, when they
got there, and couldn't possibly have been
involved.

So, my lawyer had to pay the cops more, to
tell the truth. Ole Judge Red Face, with
bulging nose got his cut too. Yeah he got
enough to keep him in liquor for a month. The
trick is to get a lawyer that knows the
judges, and goes to the same Saloon they do.
That way the lawyer can give his honor, a
donation to his reelect fund and it's Ok. If a
private citizen does that, old red face would
go crazy, and put you in the pen. I guess he
has to appear respectful, and law abiding,
especially when he is breaking the law.

At my charge dismissal hearing, I had to read
the legal papers, and sign them. Of course the
papers contained the statement that, I would
not sue the city for false arrest. I still
could not read very well, I just mumbled a
little and made it look as if I could read. I

don't think it fooled, Bulge-nose, but he had
been paid, and he went along with it. And ole
chatty was there, she smiled at him every now
and then, to soothe the nose down. The Judges
wrong head got full of blood, and he signed my
release.

Dear, lovely, Cathy was surprisingly docile,
and very civil about the whole thing. I didn't
deserve a woman of her caliber, something
needed to change. I knew it was me that had
that need. Could I do it?

Yes, I knew I was walking on thin ice where
ole Chatty was concerned. Every now and then
she would give me a stern look. I know she was
serious when she said;

"you are supposed to have character, not be
one".   I felt as if the rug, could be
pulled, from underneath me, at any second.
Walking on eggshells with some women is an
everyday thing. And at the same time, they
really go in for that; send me a rose bit.
Telling them, you love them, is supposed to
occur on an hourly basis. I really did, care
for Cathy so I made a supreme effort to lay
off the Juice.

I was a slave to the grape but, the grape is a

cruel master. The little demon in the inside of the jug demanded more and more, from me. But at the same time it caused me to have less and less to give. I recalled something about a snowball in hell idea. Damn mean ole Grape.

The lawyer that represented me at the hearing had told Ole red Face that I was looking for work. Later in the week, the old Judge called me, and asked me to help him trim the trees at his house. I said yes I would be there Saturday morning. As the morning wore on, while we worked at tree trimming, it got sort of warm. Ole Judge wanted to take a break, and what did he offer me to drink? A damn Beer, that's what. He must have wanted me to be back at his court, and to donate more money to him. That mangy dog knew, what had gotten me in jail, in the first place, Booze. Damn Mean judge.

Chapter 5

I knew getting a job was the best thing to do. I am a good mechanic, and I looked for that work. After a search, I got a job with Auto repair business. My workload was, servicing the Air condition units in the cars. This was summer and hot weather so the place was swamped, with people wanting to have their A/C fixed. The boss said when they line up, just go out and, lift the hood, hang a set of A/C gauges on the motor. That makes them think you are doing something to their car, and they won't drive off. It works out to be the same as stand in line, and take a number. The costumers will wait, because they now have some hope of driving a cool car. And I was learning to read a little, it helps, to understand, the repair manuals.

I reviewed what I had recently learned about the subject of reading; if you can read it is ok to be a drunken Judge, with a big nose. But knowing that didn't help me in everyday life, I needed to find an edge.

I kept noticing that many of the Auto Shop costumers had the same faraway look in their gaze. I couldn't quite place what could have

made them look that way. I did realize they
all had seen some, of the same experiences,
but what was that far away gaze all about.
Maybe they had been in the military at some
point. It was a look of them, having been
tamed. It was a tamed look, plus a little more
than that. The "you're in the army now", look
was never that strong. They looked something
like the crew, in my recent stay in the
crossbar hotel. Only these guys had a deeper,
concerned look. Oh well it was probably
nothing to worry about.

This bunch of good ole boys at work, really
liked to go fishing on weekends, and holidays.
And camping out was all part of it. We would
load up an old pickup and stop at the beer and
liquor store on the way. That's how I got back
to drinking again. It wasn't so bad at first
but the habit grew, and it grew more. Once
again, I was a slave to the Grape, Liquor, and
the Hops-Barley slop. Dam that little demon
was back after me. Why would a man, that had
heaven in his arms, choose to descend into the
hell, that drinking brings on? It is
unbelievable, the pull, that booze has. Dear
Chatty didn't mind a little nip here and

there, it was the, lying around drunk, act, she didn't like. Who, could blame her, I wouldn't want to see her that way. And lying with her legs spread out, as a welcome mat.

So it went on like that for a while, work during the week and getting a, drunk-on, at the weekend forays. I always managed to be somewhat presentable when I came home from a "Fishing trip". I think Chatty asked once or twice about any fish that were caught. Of course, I had to tell a stretcher, and say we ate them at the campfire. This weekend stuff was really getting to be a habit, a bad habit. Was I going to be able to stay straight, I didn't know.

The owner-Boss, where we worked, was a real boozer, two quarts of Whiskey a day. He didn't get drunk like most people did; just every now and then it showed a little. And he didn't mind if the employees drank, just wait till noon, or a little after. Having a full schedule repairing the Auto Air problems, luckily I didn't have much time to drink during the day. So Cathy and me did alright together, for a while.

Now every weekend the Auto Shop crew were ready willing and able to "Go fishing", and get another, drunk-on.

The man that owned the business was a zoo keeper, sort of. He had a small Japanese ape, and a grown Black Bear. Also, he kept assorted household pets, dogs, cats, Parrots, Raccoons.

 The bear stayed at the shop in its cage, with some resident winos, that slept around back, and looked after things at night. All day long the monkey and bear drank the beers that people would bring them. And that little ape would get hopped-up and go visit the neighboring business. One of his favorite places to go was a hamburger stand down the road. When he saw a sack of food ready for the customers, he would grab it and run back to the auto shop. Mr. Ape would go on the

 Robbery-shoplifting forays and take what he wanted. If the victims followed him and demanded money, the boss would pay them. Otherwise, he got off scot-free.

With examples like that, my suds, and fermented Grape drinking picked up too. As it turned out that small ape, and the Dog were in love, yes, in love. A black guy named Henry that worked there started to pet the dog. The ape jumped up, and was in a threatening posture. The ape had a look that said, "I am going to eat you alive if you move".

Then the dog started to growl at the man, who just wanted to pet him. Henry had them both on him, nearly going for the kill. Luckily, we got the situation under control before any blood was shed. I did not know two different species of animals could form that kind of bond, but they did. It was love no doubt. The ape, would give the dog, a helping hand, every now and then. Yeah, what you are thinking is what it did.

In the evenings when time permitted, Chatty would sing me my reading lessons. It was still difficult to learn how to read, while in the cups. Sweet Chatty didn't let on, that she knew of the increase, in my drinking she also liked to have a glass or two, with dinner. So it evened out, for a while.

I had a dental appointment, and I was very leery of the needles and pliers they used, somewhat afraid you might say. So I figured a few shots of whiskey would calm me down, it did. The dentist, I found out later, was an

ex-con. It was a Doctor recommended by my
employer. The dental doctor said my jaw tooth
had to go, that very day. When he was putting
the pliers into my mouth, his hand was shaking
a lot. I looked up at him and said, "Damn are
you sure your sober"?
He replied, "Yeah I bet it is sore".
However, he did a good job of it so I was glad
to have it over with. I headed on back to
work.
The tooth experience had me distracted and I
guess I was speeding a little. A cop thought
so, and pulled me over. Then the usual
happened, he smelled the booze, that had I
drank earlier, to kill the tooth pain. And
that did it. My mouth was still numb from the
Novocain the dentist used and I could not talk
plain. Well naturally, Mister Cop declared I
was drunk, and jailed me for driving while
drunk. This was really getting to be a drag. I
knew it was curtains for me again. The other
jail mates provided some entertainment while I
was there.
One guy had a heel on his boot that twisted,
and held some hashish. The metal foil he saved
from a diner, his girlfriend had brought,

served as a pipe. I don't think it really
mattered to him where he was; he had pleasant
dreams, for a while anyway.

It knew that it was none of my business, but a
young Mexican guy was there and didn't have a
shirt on. He was shaking from cold. And I
really don't know why, but when I saw a guy
with two blankets, I grabbed one and gave it
to the cold man. The two blanket man, started
to protest, I said to him, "Hey don't be a hog
that man is cold let him have one."

I guess we were all confused by what I did,
everyone just sat down and went back to
brooding. No fights this time, and I was glad
of that too. Well hell here I was again, in
jail maybe headed for prison.

Chapter 6

I didn't know, but I guessed my life with dear Cathy was probably over. Even though she had served me wine at the evening meal, and falsely accused me of being passed out on her couch that time. I held no grudges, and still wanted to be with her. But, I guessed she would say, sigh-a-na-rah, you hop head. And who could blame her, I was a hop headed, Wino. Every hour that went by, was filled with regret; there was no peace in my soul. Why oh why did I trade love and warmth of a good woman for the cold hearted curse of that damn little demon? It was really crazy.

One of the cellmates had a good education; I saw some possibilities of learning, more of my reading lessons.

Some people go to a insurance co. and take out a, Life insurance policy. Well Ole Larry, One of the cellmates claimed he sold Wife-Insurance policies. I had never heard of that before. It looked like; I had some time on my hands so to speak, so I listened to his story. First I questioned him to be sure I had heard him correctly;

"Say Larry, Do you really mean Wife Ins".
"Yes", he assured me that is what he meant.
"Well, how does that help anything", I asked.

I smelled a rat but there were many things I had missed by being illiterate, so I listened to him. He said it worked fairly well until he hit a string of professional, "Get-married-get-gone artists."
They demanded to be paid on their policies, or else. This guy Larry, telling the story had a look, as serious as, grave yard dead on his face. I asked what was so bad about that, paying off on, a few policies.
Then he explained; "I also had insured that, we would pay the alimonies if there was any. It got to adding it up, and it amounted to more than I could make in a lifetime. And I had to do something."
"Is that why you are in here" I asked.
He said, "Yes someone took a few, of the ex-wives down to Mexico and sold them, in a life of slavery. They somehow think it was me who

did that evil deed." Then in a humble voice
he added; "but I am innocent."

I couldn't read, but I wasn't a complete fool.
Taking no chances with him, I slid over to the
other side of the cage. If the Cops saw me
talking to him they might try to say I was
part of his Gang. I had my own troubles, it
looked better to stay away from, ole white
collar Crime, and insurance guy. I had to
avoid that man for sure.

Waiting for a hearing was a hard way to
travel. It's like sitting in a broken down
car, waiting for some help. You know it won't
help much, but you try to believe there is,
some hope anyway. Hope is what keeps the
little thought-demons in line. Without any
hope at all, the Demons take over your mind.
It is better to fool yourself somewhat, so you
can avoid, the little demon punks.

I managed to get out of Jail on Bond. Now I
had to try and get another job, that's all
there was to it. The temptation to drink, at
the Auto shop was more than I could handle.
And I had to get away from there.

The next episode coming up was pretty much
the last straw.

The Auto Shop boss and me were in a boat, at
the lake, doing some fishing. The fish weren't
biting but the mosquitoes were. Nothing
unusual about that, it was how it always
worked out. What was, unusual about it? The
small ape came swimming up to the boat and got
in. Deciding he wanted a beer, so he took mine
right out of my hand. I didn't want to give it
up but that determined look it had, told me;
in a second or two, the damn thing would be
eating my face. Quickly weighting my options,
I decided my face was worth more than that
half can of warm beer. The ape won that round,
and then he started to pick my shirt pocket
for tobacco. Again it gave me the, I am going
to kill you look. The ape won round two also.
There was no other choice, trying to fight off
a deranged, drunk ape in a small boat, was an
experience I did not want. He settled down to
drinking beer and chewing my cigarettes, and
was peaceful again. I wanted to avoid that
ape, if I could, so I turned around and went
back to fishing. Damn mean ape.
So all that drinking and things like that,
added up to me looking for some other line of
work. I had been thinking along this line for

a while now and it came to a head. I had found out about that far away look many of the usual customers wore. The real spacey looking ones that came by regularly, it turned out they were all ex-cons. And they came by to see the Boss because was an ex-con too. I decided I wanted to be an ex-employee, and not an ex-con.

Chapters 7

Well I did quit the auto shop and wanted
get another job. And wouldn't you know it, I
picked a time when the national economy was in
a recession. What could I do now?

I met an old drunk, and he was a tree trimmer.
We would go driving around, in some of the
better neighborhoods, knocking on doors. That
was how we got work, some times. I had bought
a gasoline chain saw, and he had the knowhow,
so we split the money we got. I learned tree
trimming from him as well as the firewood
business. A lot of hard work, but I had to
live and I was no thief. That's the way it
went, for a while, and what could go wrong
with all that hard work?

Ever-Clear, is a drink that they sell, in
liquor stores. It's almost 95% alcohol. It's
so powerful it curls your toes, and produces a
loud ringing in the ears. One small spoonful
is more than enough. But of course me being a
true al-key I used it to excess. The cops said
my truck ran over a guy's boat, I don't think

I did but, wasn't sure. Everything had gone black, just like walking around at night with your eyes closed. Well of course I was back in Jail doing time. Cognitive decline; was that what was happening to me? Well of course it was, the alcohol burns your brain for fuel. That's what powers up, the "High" brought on by the alcohol. There is nothing free in this world, everything cost something. If you change any mater into, another state of mater, there is a price.

Sometimes I had got to watch public TV, where a person learns things like that. It seemed to me the other stations helped bring on the decline. They did that, by not requiring a person to think, all you need do is look. TV is a narcotic, in and of, it's self. Not as strong as drugs but, mind numbing, just the same. And you stay in a state of confusion, just like drugs. The people that watch sports, know ever time their hero did anything. But can't tell you why the national debt is choking the population to death. Or more importantly who added the most to that debt. Well do you? Rah! Rah! Rah! sis- boom- ba But right now I had other problems, like finding a way out of the cross bar hotel, where I was doing time. This time it wasn't so bad, they let me out in two days. They said because I wasn't actually driving when they saw me there was not D.U.I. charge. It was only a drunk in public charge. Guess my truck didn't run over that guy's boat after all. They kept that old truck, the impound fee was more than it was worth.

Going back to my old hideout in the ruins, I spent some time thinking. And remembered that cute idea; I had heard someone say before. If you can't do the time—don't do the crime. So I decided to go straight, and do some time working, while I was sober. That seemed the right thing to do.

I worked hard, and saved enough to get set up with an apartment, and some good transportation. Now I was ready to enter into the position of productive citizen. Yes my reading had progressed to where I could fill out a job application. And went seeking work as a Machinist, a good trade to be in. I knew I had to establish a work record of being on time and, not missing any days. Since the laying around drunk act, was now kept to a minimum, my health improved. And you need your heath to go to work every day. Well that might seem simple and it is. But it the small things like that, drunks don't seem to grasp. When a person is loaded, and breathing out, 100 proof fumes, he don't think very good at all. That was something else that occurred to me now. It seemed I was, doing a lot of lately; thinking.

Chapter 8

I started to wonder if it might help me to
seek some spiritual guidance, I went to a
church. It was an old movie theater. The
reverend was a woman and she really did
perform. She had a microphone with a three
hundred foot, extra-long cord. And she was
slowly walking up the aisle going on with her
sermon. I don't remember what it was now, but
I thought of something funny, and gave sort of
a chuckle. I didn't mean any disrespect, but
it must have looked that way. During one of
her pauses, one of my chuckles got out, bad
move. Preacher woman came running, up the
aisle and stopped in front of me. I tried to
slink down into the chair but could not get
far enough down into it. The reverend let go
with some of the "You're going to hell stuff",
I could not blame her. She thought it was me
just being mean. The only thing that made
sense was get out the door, so out the door I

went. No angel wings, but flying anyway.
Trudging on back to my apartment and resting
up from, a night at the theater was my goal. I
really was sorry for what happened but I could
not change it. Then, remembering that was
part of the serenity prayer. Having the wisdom
to know what could be undone and what
couldn't.
So maybe praying would be of help to me, when
I was trying to stay,
"Juice-less". It was certainly worth a try,
and more than one try too. Well enough of
that for the time being I had to get my rest,
big day tomorrow, at the salt mine. That's
what I called that job I had, going to the
salt mine. But it wasn't that bad, it was
worse. I liked the work but the conditions
were a bit harsh. In the adjoining building,
was an aluminum smelter? They melted down
scrap metal and molded Bar-B-Que char
broilers.
The shop I worked in was mighty oily, and we
used the red cloth hand wipes. In the morning
the towels lying on the work bench, would be
bright blue. I think it was the P.H. or
something like that. I knew the air couldn't

be safe to breathe.

I had a slip-up on my drinking one evening.
The next, morning, still hung over, I went in
to work, earlier than usual. I went to see the
metal melting workers; I swear I thought I had
entered some room, in hell. They were all
around the smelting fire and had dirty faces.
And of course when someone new entered the
work area; they looked to see who it was. With
my hung-over booze induced mindset, it
certainly looked like a gang of mean devils.
Yes I thought I had accidently opened the door
to hell. And that thankfully that scene helped
me curb my drinking for a while. I had to get
away from there it might really be a part of
ole bezel-bubs workshop. Amen

Chapter 9

I had heard that driving a truck was a swell way to see this beautiful country of ours. And it would be a chance to be around some sober people. So truck driving school is where I went next. The instructor was a little bit weird; he liked to scream the lessons to be learned. After going at an idle, around the obstacles course for about a week, it was time to get on the road. We hooked up a loaded trailer, and lined up for our morning driving lessons. Mr. Holler-Loud, asked who wanted to go first. We students were all nervous about going out on the highway, for the first time, in the big Truck. I was scared stiff, but I knew if I didn't speak up right then, I might quit the school.

"I will go first" I said. So off we go, onto the highway. I had all of about 3 hour's total, learning to shift the ten forward gears, and no time at all with a 52 foot trailer behind. My mind was whirling with excitement, trying to judge the distance and speed of the approaching traffic. After all I didn't want to get us all killed. So out on the road I went, and of course I missed the next gear. The instructor screamed at the top of his voice, "&&&### &&&**% "I aint going to put up with this".

 He must be crazy I thought, I wonder if he thinks that screaming act, would help matters. I don't know why he couldn't see that he was taking my attention from the task at hand. It was a heavy load on my mind. I was trying to drive a huge machine, that I knew almost nothing about, dodging the traffic, and looking

at a crazy man, screaming at me. That
was some experience to say the least.

 But I did manage to get in the right
lane, and roll on down the road. And
every second that went by it was getting
easier. I started to get the feel of the
mammoth sized truck, and learning what
to expect from the controls. So that was
my first day learning to read while
driving a truck. I was reading the
street signs. And there was, a lot of
street signs to read. As usual there
were 6 students in the truck at a time.
Ole nut head would scream him-self
hoarse, I figured. He had 6 member
captured audience to holler at.

One of the students was going up a steep
hill, he missed a gear. He didn't know
to do with the heavy giant truck.

 We were all in the back praying, that
we didn't go off the cliff. We were
praying because, when you miss shift,

the large trucks, it not so simple, to get it into another gear. Well there we were stopped, headed up a very steep hill, with a nervous student driver, that didn't know how to get the truck safely going again. All the boys in the back knew if old stupid went to screaming our goose was cooked. The newbie driver would probably let it roll off the embankment. Then a miracle occurred. Old screamer calmly told the student how to get up the hill, and we did.

We guessed that hollering son of a gun, finial realized, what an impact his loud mouth was having on the students. But no, he didn't learn, to not do that hollering yet.

There was a large Black man, a little over 6 foot, two hundred fifty pounds of muscle, in our class. We were going out for more driving, on another day. I have

forgotten what the man did wrong
something minor. But crazy man screamed
at him. The large black man looked at
the teacher; I thought the screamer, was
a dead man. But after staring at him, in
a manner that said he, would be a dead
man, if he did that anymore, we went on.
There was no more screaming that day. We
had all long since thought the teacher
was afraid to go out, with us driving.
And we though he was like a hysterical
female and couldn't control his
emotions, so we mostly ignored his
hollering.

We could now control the huge truck a
little better so that part of our nerves
was calmed down. If the teacher wanted
to act like a woman, well we would let
him. And little by little, we learned
how to drive and park the truck and
trailer. Everything is slowed down while
driving a large truck that is the way it

seems, and is. Only after it gets to
cruising speed, it starts to feel more
like a car. The road speed has to match
the engine Rpm's, or it won't go into
the selected gear. It take coordination
and the feel to do it right.
When we went to the state office, to get
our Commercial driving license, I was
driving. We stopped at a stop sign, I
don't remember why, but ole nutty
screamed at me. I gave him the, I am
going to kill you look, and I think it
would have happened. But I managed to
only say, "Don't do that no more".
And the surprising thing was he didn't
scream at me after that. So we all got
our new commercial driving license, and
were glad of that. But we all still had
a lot more of training to go thru.
Safety meeting and how to do the paper
work that was required. And then we
would each go on the road with an

experienced driver for more training. We had to learn how to read. There were the highway signs of course, but more than that. We had to learn how to read the road, and if going down a steep mountain, how to get to the bottom alive. Yes my education was progressing in a satisfactory manner, and I am so glad I learned how to read. I hopped some day to get back together with my sweet Chatty Cathy, but it would take a lot of work on my part.

Ebooks, Audio Books, and Printed Books
Available on Amazon

Other Books by William Ardrey

Wade Explains Ranch Life

The Old Cowboys: Love To Make Money

Star Truck

How I got Fat

Learning To Read

The Old Cowboys: We Go North

My Very Good Luck

Red Meat: The Doctor

Poetry From The Dark

The Big Bang Revisited

Gold Wolf

The Wrath Of The Grapes

The Trouble Shooters

Sadie Glory City

scraperbill@yahoo.com

William Ardrey

Thank You For Your Support